D1553933

Little Feasts

Stories by

Jules Archer

Little Feasts

ISBN: 978-1-7345158-0-0

Cover design and interior image by Carolyn Brandt

Printed in the U.S.A.

For more titles and inquiries, please visit:

www.thirtywestph.com

The Menu

Little Feasts

In-N-Out Doesn't Have Bacon

I know she fucked the tree. A weeping willow; our yard; flushed, throes of passion; a guttural moan on its invisible lips. My sister passes by the window, wiggles her fingers, blows it a brazen kiss.

I scowl. I imagine the bills I'll get from having to call an arborist to deal with the upturned roots, and a therapist to deal with my stress about my sister's expulsion from college and her strange obsession with boudoir botany.

"What are you doing?" I ask.

Maria's grin is a blossom of mischievousness. "Flirting."

My sister loves nature. Succulents, fiddle-leaf fig trees, red bamboo — none are safe. She's naturally drawn to the flora of life, has been ever since she was a baby when she took to sucking on vines instead of bottles. Nights, she cloaks herself in ivy, claims she can grow flowers in her palm.

I watch her fondle a potted viola. "Get ready for dinner." I check my watch. She's still in her grubby green bathrobe.

"He'll be here at eight."

"Groovy." Soil sifts between her long fingers.

"Go, Maria."

"I'll go, Catherine."

Maria lets loose of the plant and moves for the stairs. I sink into the armchair, rub my brow. I think of later tonight. Of after dinner. Of bacon. Of a drive-thru and In-N-Out Burger. Of silently eating in my car while my sister sleeps.

Tom stares at Maria. He hasn't touched his tempeh. His tongue has practically red-carpet-rolled out his mouth like a cartoon wolf.

Tom's a very handsome clerk from work. Cheekbones like glass, eyes like burnt charcoal, his fingers fly fast across the keyboard and I take my lust out by setting him up with my sister. They're the same age, both beautiful and young — and their breath always smells better than average. Secretly, I love him, but I'm older, and I've been told I'm too sad to satisfy a man and am only recently free to date again.

"Delicious," Tom says, breaking the silence to ooze enthusiasm. "I can't believe it's not real meat. I'd serve this every damn day if I could."

Maria nods. Her long braids plaited with backyard weeds sway. "I know, right?"

I watch Tom chew the gummy piece of faux meat. He hates it. But still, he eats it — eats it for Maria who's chowing down on her fat slice of tempeh like it's a Butterfinger bar.

Across the room, I stare at a picture of my dead husband — mowed down by a drunk driver. Maria was the only one who said nothing those torturous long months, who never wondered when I'd snap out of it, who'd only shriek at others when they asked me how I was coming along. Maria's shrieks got well-practiced after her two-month stint at the psych hospital. I'm the one who got her out, years ago, against our mother's wishes, so maybe we owed each other something. Maybe we're just sisters. Maybe we are each other's protection.

Maria floats a warm smile to Tom. "We must adjourn for a mere moment." When she stands, she nearly bows. I bet he loves that. He's never had a woman bow to him before. I bet he's popping a boner right now beneath the table.

We meet in the kitchen. Still, within earshot, we whisper among the china cabinet and our dead mother's beloved Hummel figurines.

"What's going on, Cat? You barely touched your food." I roll my eyes. She doesn't want to talk about boys. She wants to talk about how I'm not showing her plant-based meal enough love.

"I have plans later."

"You burger-loving bitch," she swears, socking my arm.

I laugh. "What do you think about Tom?"

Maria shrugs. "You can have him," she says and flaps a lazy hand. "He's not my type." She eyes the window. She's already flushed, her eyes on the crooked fern out back.

Tom smells like corn nuts and sawdust. I imagine telling Maria this, and her sigh of exasperation is enough to kill me dead on the spot.

He leans up onto his elbow, rolls off the condom. I stay under the sheets, stare at the ceiling.

"So, your sister," he says. "You don't think she's interested or..."

The question hangs in the hair like a noosed body.

I want to say something to take his mind off Maria, to disgust him, to make him notice me - my small face, my awkward body - so, stomach clenching, hands twisting sheet corner, I say, "My sister fucks plants."

Tom flops onto his back, his eyes wide and unblinking. "Fascinating."

I watch his erection throb against the sheet.

"In-N-Out," I say, suddenly wanting him out of the house and away from Maria. "Can you drive me? I need a bacon cheeseburger."

Tom's handsome brow furrows. In another life, he'd be a politician. "In-N-Out doesn't have bacon."

I roll over onto my side. I needle the bridge of my nose, needle it into oblivion. "Jesus, Tom. You're just full of bad fucking news, aren't you?"

Hours later, I arrive home, fed and fat. I find Maria in the kitchen, sitting on the floor, eating leftovers.

"You smell like meat," she says, tracing my darkened silhouette with her fork.

"Tell me about it," I say, joining her on the floor. My stomach feels greasy from the burger, from Tom, from some strange artificial sense of connection. My husband and I never used condoms. I just sloppy-second-screwed the office temp. All I want is to eat and to fuck and I can't even do that right. Hunger never felt so hard.

Together, we sit shoulder to shoulder in silence. Maria smells of wild clover, of honeysuckle. We listen to the whisper of trees across the street. She curls her hand around mine, passes something soft, something quiet. I open my palm: freshly-grown Morning Glory. I must squint to believe it. That we are both alive.

How to Love a Monster with Average-Sized Hands

If I could marry a myth it would be monstrous, but not monstrous like frightening — monstrous as in a monstrous love where I'd be prouder than a Phoenix in plumage, and hotter than a poker. I'd swing on Cthulhu's feelers. Take a water-slide ride down the tail of Godzilla. I'd let a Wendigo eat my heart and put a ring on it and drive me out to our small town's overlook where he'd insist I'd wear protection and let me finish the rest of my wine. Loch Ness monster? More like Loch Bless monster, because every night you come to me in bed is another day I fall in love. Instead of calling the cops, my father would shake hands with Cyclops, and call him the son he never had, because if your face was a little more lion and a little less wolf we'd have a magically monstrous love on our hands, but instead I am stuck with you, and you are no creepy cryptid but a mere under-the-bed boogeyman that sends me screaming, only that's what I get for having married a monster with average-sized hands and not looking out the front door before answering it.

Hard to Carry and Fit in a Trunk

Ginny Hanover always envisioned herself as a slender-boned girl.

Hell, she always envisioned herself in the trunk of a car so right off the bat, something's wrong with this scenario.

She wants that frail, swan-like neck; bony bird arms. She wants to be lifted, crisscrossed over shoulders, bound and gagged. She can rip Duct tape in two. She's practiced. Her full-throttle scream is at the ready.

It's odd. She knows this. She's told her shrink this. Dr. Donna Marjoram (it's a spice, not a maiden name) listens. Puts pen to paper. Nods. It's impressive how she manages to keep her eyes from bulging when Ginny tells her the fantasies she keeps.

Ginny rips napkins apart while she watches the Investigation Discovery channel. It's nerve-wracking: the ones who get taken, who are easily lifted and never found again. She's covetous.

She's prey. Or she would be if she could drop those last fifty pounds. Ginny eats chocolate pudding precisely at eight in the pm. Licks spoons laden with whipped cream. Uses tortillas as plates.

Ginny's tried Weight Watchers and those awful slim shakes, but she just can't drop the pudge. She exercises, too. Long jogs taken at dark times. Conveniently forgets her cell phone at home. Fills her cats' food bowls before leaving the house. She walks down on the train tracks, deep in the heart of downtown, offering herself. But no one wants a fat girl.

No one will take her. All the Jim's and John's and Jeffrey's she's met with penchants for sickly ambitions, and they still leave her be. No one trolls her in the dark, tires peeling down lonely streets. She doesn't carry mace or pack heat or sport a rape whistle. And yet, she's still not the appealing sort. A waif to sling into a van.

She wants to be equal. The youth and the thin win at everything, even if they're ugly. She's not ugly, but she's fat, and this means Ginny won't get the thrill of the chase. The thrill of being stranded with - stalked by - a stranger. The thrill of heart-pumping adrenaline and sweaty palms. Oh, the dreams she has.

A life-long dream. She doesn't know why she wants it. Maybe too many hours watching horror movies and dissecting stray dogs in her backyard and letting her brother's hands choke her throat. It's why she got fat, but it's also why she wants to get thin.

Catch-22's are sons-of-bitches. Ginny knows this. She's fat-girl Ginny, and no one will ever have their illicit way with her. She's harder to carry. It's not fair. All things should be equal in love and warped visions.

Ginny thinks back to her favorite movie: *The Silence of the Lambs*. Pasty-faced Jame Gumb and that hole in the floor. The lucky chosen. Girls with patterns drawn on their backs, puffy flesh, and round, round ankles. They are her aspirations.

Before Ginny sleeps at night she always wonders why it can't be her. Pines for equality. Oh, Buffalo Bill, ye who likes them thick and large and juicy. Like steaks. Hefty women who could fill Hefty bags.

The Ice Cream Cone

In the horror movie, you are being chased by a man. Of course, it's a man — a man in a mask to hide his face, the cowardly devil. You see him coming over the hedge, fat and shaky like whale blubber, and you wonder how he can catch you. But when he lands like a perfect-ten gymnast (because this is a horror movie) you take one last lick of your ice cream cone; say *okay, fine*; gutter-bomb it; run. As you run, your sparkly-girl life flashes in front of your eyes: the boy in high school sticking his sneakered foot in your crotch beneath your conjoined desks, unasked, and rubbing you to frisson (*ugh ugh ugh*); the boy in grade school laughing and slapping your ass next to the lockers while his peon friends looked on; your mother's boyfriend who, upon smelling your Bath and Body Works Cucumber Melon lotion, smiled, licked his lips and said, *hmm, something sure smells good*, and you were skeeved out because you recently saw a documentary on scent and how Cucumber Melon means arousal and now you can never look at him in the face again; your mother's second boyfriend who knocked her into a wall and she left you to fend for herself while she shuttered herself in the bathroom — and while all these memories are terribly sad, they are not necessarily terribly bad because they remind you that you have faced worse things in life that are not horror-movie related, and in each scenario, you did not run; you learned; and what you are learning now is that — surprise! — because this is a horror movie, you forgot you still have an ice cream spoon in your hand, perfect for scooping the guts out of trash men. So, you stop, turn, wait for him to run into you, and — without hesitation — poke the man in his stomach with the pink spoon. Just a little poke, but it works; he opens up. He wails like all pathetic villains do and crumple into a pile, his steamy, snakey guts spilling out as he tries to cuddle them back to his body like a tiny, warm baby. You smile, and when you turn around the ice cream man is there, his white hat tipped, a cone triple stacked with mint chocolate chip, and you think *cool, bro,* and take it, because you've already slain the dragons today and nothing else has tasted this nice.

Guerilla Drive-In

It all starts at the drive-in. He sucks her toes.

The night's hot and dark. She's thankful he can't see her face. They keep the windows rolled up and the radio going. Some Willie Nelson song drones on about a girl with blue eyes. Beads of sweat trail from the top of her collarbone to her bellybutton. They pool there, raindrops collecting in a pond. If she shifts, they'll spill. She turns her head, pressing a hand against the image of the movie projected on the backseat window.

He starts slurping on the big toe of the right foot; the left foot finished. She feels his tongue - a big, wet slippery eel - wrap around and tug, lick, lap, like her toes, are a snow cone. She thinks about this. A snow cone would be refreshing in this heat. Take her mind off the slobbering man kneeling on the floorboard below her.

Maybe cherry flavored.

She shuts her eyes, stretching back against the door. He's on the pinky toe now. Almost done. She imagines how she looks; legs sprawled out, propped like she's giving birth. The man wedged on the floor; face turned toward her. No officer, he's not eating pussy; he's eating toes.

She giggles and the sweat spills. Tendrils of cool liquid run down her sides, wetness collecting on the Naugahyde seat beneath her. The man raises his head, an eyebrow.

"What was your name again?"

"Violet." She draws her legs back, fluffs her skirt. "It's my turn."

He nods.

She crawls into the front seat and shoves the cigarette lighter into its socket. There's a sigh from behind her and a squeak of the seat as the man moves into place. The handle pops. Removing it, she holds it up, out, the burning ember end glowing orange.

The man offers her his arm. She wipes sweat from her neck, her chest. It's hot.

The Lie Tree

"Go out to the Lie Tree," Daddy would always say.

No matter the size of the whopper, us kids marched down the dusty back road, across fallen leaves and prairie dog holes, to the stately pecan tree, its twisted branches beckoning the sky. Sometimes, if the lies were really bad, we were forced to crawl the half-mile on our hands and knees until we reached roots. Later, when the scabs hardened, we'd pick them off and feed them to the chickens.

One day, Daddy said he'd chop that tree down and peel away the layers of sable-colored bark so we could see our lies imprinted on the smooth flesh beneath. Daddy said lies always clung. Stained your skin like they stained this here tree.

Mama lied when she met Daddy. Told him she was already with child, and then she was. He thought her name was Clara up until the day Joey was born. And then she whispered in his ear, amid the squalling baby and cigarette smoke-stained air, "The name's Celeste."

"I hate it," Bud said, kicking at its roots. He ground his grubby little fists up and punched the air in front of the Lie Tree.

"Brushing your teeth, Bud, it ain't that hard to do," Joey said, ashing a cigarette.

Sitting on the ground, I drew knees into my chest. "You're gonna get busted for that, ya know."

"Dad does it." Joey shrugged. "C'mon, Bud, out with it. We ain't got all day."

Lip trembling, Bud whispered his lie to the tree. Bark grew underneath his fingernails as he gripped its sides and held tight. Bud started to cry, and Joey patted the top of his bowed head.

I kept my mouth shut and thought about everything the tree knew about me.

The butterscotch-colored vinyl of Daddy's that I scribbled my name on again and again in black Sharpie.

Grape juice spilled on a couch cushion, flipped over to conceal the evidence.

Sneaking out of the house to join Marcie Cummings at a senior party where we both kissed the same boy.

Trying to pass off six beers as two.

Rob, and just where, exactly, his hands have been.

"Clementine, be mine," Rob rhymed. He had a rhyme for everyone in town. "Betty from 'bama, fresh from the 'slama." "June, June, take me to the moon."

Rob wore an eyepatch over his right eye and painted hand-lettered signs for local business establishments. He wrote poems on telephone poles across our town. His bad eye hurt, but only on days when it rained.

Pressing my hand against his patch, my legs wrapped around his waist, Rob lifted and backed me up against the Lie Tree. Bark flaked, rubbed off with our up and down motions, tickling the small of my back and leaving long scratches.

Paint-stained fingers in my hair, Rob kissed my cheek, said, "I could punch you through drywall, Clem."

Mama said we were born into a family of liars: people who couldn't tell the truth even if there were pliers gripping their tongues and bamboo shoots under their fingernails. "It's in your genes," she'd claim, and I'd check the pockets of my Wranglers to make sure I wasn't carrying around any of our family taint.

When Joey lied about skipping school to fish the Canoochee, he was made to live under the Lie Tree for two days in the dead of summer. I tried to smuggle out a pitcher of water but was stopped at the door. Daddy's biceps bulged as he crossed his arms and pointed me back toward the kitchen.

Joey got sick a few days later but no one ever said anything about that.

When the world took Mama, her tombstone read *Clara*. It made me wonder if Daddy had always loved her more: the woman who had lied to him first.

I'd guess at the lies Daddy would tell the tree. Because he sent himself down there, too. Can of suds in his hand, shoulders hunched. He'd always return home red-faced and crying about Mama, his shaky hands sloppily reaching for a hug from one of us kids. He'd sit us on his lap, say he loved us, and we'd repeat the same words back. Those nights were the good kind of nights. Where no one ever got in trouble for their lies.

Rob told me to do the one honest thing I'd done since birth.

Rolling out of his arms, I said, "I haven't been honest since birth."

I practiced a lie to the Lie Tree before telling it to Daddy. Ran a finger down one of its long roots, chipped off a piece of rough bark and stuck it in the pocket of my jeans before crawling back to the house and telling him I'd be home for dinner.

Far, far away Rob took me from the Lie Tree. Far away from the town in a busted, rusted, gassed-up station wagon.

One hundred miles traveled and four oatmeal cream pies polished off, I leaned across the bucket seat and cupped Rob's jaw, held his bad eye under a soft palm. I wriggled closer, closer until his paint-stained hand clutched my thigh and told him.

"The name's Cassandra."

Prettier Things

Every Sunday, I drink a glass of orange juice while secretly watching my next-door neighbor cut the grass. I peer through my kitchen window, angling the blinds *just so*. He mows in a tight white tank top, stained pits, biceps glistening in the sun. But those aren't my favorite. What I really like are his forearms. They bulge when he paces the lawn, his meaty hands wrapped tight around the lawn mower handle. The muscle moves, snake-like, underneath taut skin, dark arm hair.

His name is Bob.

Bob's a friendly man. Moved into the house across the street this summer. Much more fun to watch than Mrs. Pritchett fighting to straighten her arthritic stockings. Bob's a mechanic, hands oiled up with grease, the cuticles black. He's always working in his driveway, the tops of his feet visible as he tinkers on the undersides of cars and trucks.

I wave to him when I check my mail each afternoon. He lifts a hand in salute sometimes motioning to my car, letting me know the tires are low. He always fills them when I forget to take the car in.

I spy on him.

He picks up trash when he jogs, puts it in his pocket for throwaway later.

He puts out a bowl of milk on his porch for stray cats. I press a hand to my heart.

He plays a game of stickball with the kids who live down the block, pretends to steal second base and lifts Jimmy Miller high into the air when the kid scores a run. Walks them home when it gets dark.

I pass him in the supermarket. I buy pickles and TV dinners while he buys bags of ice and stamps.

Bob's thoughtful.

He comes over to my house to tell me my roof might need some work. He noticed it last week. He hands me my mail. We talk on the porch. I offer him a glass of lemonade, but he declines. He rests a palm against the side of the house as we talk. It leaves a grease mark.

I let it stay there, counting whorls on fingertips.

The house he's renting keeps its blinds drawn. The yard immaculate. Sprinklers come on at five every evening. I sip iced tea with lemon and sit on my porch, tanning my legs.

Bob brings back the ladies. He's skilled that way.

Once a month, a platinum head glimmers in the dark. In his busted Chevy, he drives them to his place. They're always blonde with pert breasts and noses. I watch from my window as he takes them inside. Lights flash on in the house and then go dark mere seconds later. I never see the women leave.

I tug at my own ink-colored strands.

I make an appointment with my hairdresser.

I bring the jar of pickles over to his house and ask him to open it. My hands are too weak. He wraps his worn palms around the top and twists, the lid popping in one quick snap. His forearms bulge, and I know he likes to squeeze prettier things than pickle jars.

He gives it back to me and says he likes my hair better dark. I tell him thank you.

He cleans a lot. Drags oddly-shaped packages out of his front door and into the bed of his pickup truck. He's gone for an hour or two and then returns, his boots and the hems of his jeans caked with mud. I crack my knuckles, think of a good spot remover I can recommend.

One day, I wait for him on my porch. When he emerges from his house, lugging a tightly tied trash bag behind him, I make my move. Seeing me coming, Bob raises a hand in greeting, dark grease caking his rough palms.

I hold up a thermos filled with iced coffee.

He waves it away and throws the trash bundle into the truck bed. It seems light. I follow him back to his doorstep. There's a shovel, the wood-worn handle politely resting against the side of his house. Bob opens his door — not too wide — asks me when I'll be going back to black.

I tell him he sounds like the AC/DC song and his smile is wary. Beyond and behind the mesh window of his screen door, another trash bag is tied up and waiting in the hallway. I shield my eyes against the sun, asking if he needs help. He smells like bleach.

Bob stretches a hand out. Long fingers trace my clavicle, calm fingertips prod bone. They move to my throat, make the slightest indentation to the flesh: a tender chokehold. I enjoy the tiniest flutter of color in my vision, and then it's gone. Bob says I should wear more sunscreen, my skin is too pink.

I see him around town and still spy when he mows the lawn. I admire his bulging biceps. I make myself Bloody Marys in the morning, gnashing on the celery stalks while I sprawl polka-dot-bikini-clad across my front yard on a beach towel. I let the summer sun tan my hide, wiping dripping sweat from my eyes. The insides of my thighs rub, slapping together like slices of baloney.

I practice the story I'll tell the press when the cops find him out.

But until then, he's mine.

I remove my sunglasses when he exits his house. I wave and Bob waves back, our hands lingering, knowing, in the sticky air of a sticky afternoon.

Happiness, Lies, & Reno Rush

Drive me away on your motorcycle, black like the night when it's warm, and spin us onto the freeway. Above the engine roar, you'll ask if I remembered my dress. When the sun rises, we'll reach Reno. There, you'll dance me over dizzying casino carpet because you have brought the rings and I've left behind coffee in the pot and there is no way the world can get us now. When we're pronounced, you take my face in your hands, kiss me like I'm a souvenir, and I'll close my eyes, think: *Good lord in heaven, I hope this baby's yours.*

Skillet

My mom says it's a Valentine from our ancestors: a battered big-hearted cast iron skillet. Been in the family for ages of aging women, dates back to the 19th century, has lasted through slopped-up servings of inky black bean stew, garlands of sizzling bacon, puffed-up Dutch babies.

I grip the handle of the cast iron.

Mom eyes the tilt of my wrist.

She cyclones a swirl of olive oil in the charred bottom of the pan. "It's all about technique," she says. "You meld the ingredients the way you would strike a skull — carefully."

"That's a funny way to look at it," I say, then try to lift the pan again. But I can't. It must weigh twenty pounds.

"Carefully, Annie," Mom says again. She wraps her hand around my forearm and helps me lift the pan high.

The borscht is greasy. Too greasy. I have made it so. I peer over the skillet and watch the edges of my face shimmer like oil on the soup's surface.

My sister comes in, cocks her hip.

"It smells like farts."

"You're a fart. Go on. Get out of here."

She flicks her hair and exits.

My great-great-grandmother's recipe must have missed an ingredient. I stare, frustrated, at the handwritten instructions, faded like fog on a windowsill. I turn the recipe card over. I peer closer at the final lines. *Swing high*, it says, stained with red.

After cooking, to protect it from rust, the skillet must be seasoned. Animal fat. A rub of lard, inside, outside. The curve of the skillet cool and slick beneath the paper towel, the palm of my hand. On its backside: dark, sticky stains that linger. I trace a finger over one. I compare it to a shadow. Silent, skulking, spooky with knowing. I wipe excess fat from my hands. I put the skillet in the hot oven, and hope the stickiness will burn off.

Dinner at my grandmother's house. She is craving oxtails and pork sausages. "No complaints," she says. She cooks these in the oven on a cookie sheet. As she and I wait for pig skins to crackle, she tells me about our lineage. Eight generations of women who have learned to love wrong and swing high.

One ancestor loved a Civil War soldier who asked to be put out of his one-legged misery. Another married a railroad man, but once he raised a fist to her, said nope, no more. Then there was John, the husband of my grandmother's grandmother's grandmother who was mistaken for a burglar. Then Lance, a lousy boyfriend of my aunt's who simply forgot to cap the toothpaste. And Debbie, a 1950s homemaker who, well, just didn't like her husband Thomas, or his brother Benji.

Grandmother doesn't know if it's the pan or the men we pin down, but either way, we're cursed.

I am putting on the oven mitt when she leans in. A crooked smile unfurls across her face. "It's inherited," she whispers.

I try not to agree with her.

My mother has a new lover. A man with black hair and pockmarked skin. They spoon on the couch, curve necks to shoulders. They make soft, sucking sighs. I lurk on the staircase. I watch the back of the man's head, curious about the round orbit of it, wishing I knew where all the soft spots were. No recipe card for that.

My sister comes to sit beside me on the stairs. I rub her knee. I wonder at what's inside of us because we understand now that the soft spots on the front of the face are the nasal cavity, the window of the mouth, the sockets of the eyes. Our father taught us that.

Out in the gravel driveway, I swing the skillet at the sky. It glances off the noon-blue heaven. The muscles in my arms tense, wiry and lean. My wrists have transformed into steel as I whip cast iron like a baseball bat. I hear the way it whispers my name. It says it knows me well. It promises me a true purpose.

When I straighten up to drop the pan to the grass, I see my mother on the porch. She looks different: her entire cheek bruised; the white of her eye red.

When her lover's beat-up Cadillac swerves into the drive, my mother smiles at me with all her teeth.

I pick up the pan. When I swing again, I swing carefully.

We Will Set Anything on Fire

The night they make us throw our words into the fire, we have nothing but smiles behind our hands.

The torn sheets of Merriam-Webster's Dictionary include a page that begins with "home" and ends with "homeless." An armed man with fair hair burns another: "outright/ova." An AK-47 dangles over his hip.

Reporters from the local gazette toss in snapped pencils, empty jars of ink, ancient typewriters, yellowed computers, and laptops.

A podium goes up in front of the courthouse to broadcast words of encouragement and foster community. A banner is hung: "MAY WE ALL BE WELL."

In front of me, a woman reaches into her throat. She removes her voice box. A pulpy orb in the moonlight, it is floated between hands until it reaches the pyre. There it lands, meat on a grill. When it cries out, the woman cannot hush it, so instead, she holds a finger to her lips, and now there's blood everywhere.

In line, my sister is crying. She hugs her diary. I tell her to hurry, to eat its pages — her words — one by one, so the flames can never hold them hostage. I look at the bandage on my palm, the one covering the burn from the brand. They removed my tattoo that used to say, 'I WILL NOT TELL A LIE'.

The man with the gun comes to stand beside me. He pats my head, says, "Girl, we wrote the book on the lies we tell, the words we burn, the people who are the best of the worst."

"Why?" I ask.

"Don't you know?" he says. "Your voice is a match begging for fire."

Cyberspace Soup

Some creepy dude PayPal's me $50 to watch me eat a bowl of soup. Over the webcam, he tells me to slurp it slowly. I wait for the money to hit my account, and then I do. Like a kitten's, my tongue laps languidly and long. Hot chicken broth flicks off the spoon and dots the tip of my nose. The man's fingers clench the loose fabric at the knees of his trousers. He breathes heavily through his mouth. His panting turns to moaning and the moans turn to shudders. Peak pleasure reached, I disconnect and kill the webcam.

A fetish for everything. Although, mine involves keeping clothes on. I don't even have to shave my legs. Hell, if my legacy is to become the poster child for Campbell's, so be it. My first time — my first bowl — was lentil. A bad choice for the way it sank sodden into my stomach. I remember seeing the rosy blush of my cheeks reflected back at me via video screen as the red-faced man shrugged out of his soiled underwear and jerked it to the rhythmic slurp of my tongue.

I spin around in my chair as the small space I call a bedroom is breached by the sudden appearance of my father. I darken my monitor. I smell Slivovitz and Saltines on his breath. He asks me when dinner is, asks if we will have soup. I tell him, and raise the spoon like a gavel, no we will not. He does not protest, and I smile. Tell him I will join him in a moment.

His mind, inexplicably alien these days, wavers and then clears. Tentatively, he calls me by name, questions why the paint on the wall is peeling. Both of these observations are correct. I watch as his fragile form retreats to hobble down the stairs. Though thin and lost, he is still strong in father form. And me, I am a calendar, waiting on a day where I can give him fancy things with cords and wires to heal his brain and bones.

A buzz from the computer, and I swivel. A blinking light. A notification of a promise I have not yet delivered. A cyberspace jungle where soup is to be slurped.

I rise from the chair. It's a spaghetti kind of night.

Anne Boleyn Could Drink You Under the Table

Anne Boleyn loves mead. "You drink it like a fish," Henry used to say. And how he laughed: big, baritone, besotted. But that was before she was beheaded, before she had to do it all over again.

Now she's back. A reincarnated, over-educated college student in some preppy East Coast town. She has a cramped dorm, a roommate who listens to Norwegian Black Metal, and these cool things called jeans instead of corsets and gowns. In her leisure, there is no needlecraft, only homework. Anne prefers not to listen to her professors, though. She never thought the words of others were just ways to get someone else in trouble, but now she knows differently.

She sneaks mead into the lecture halls, sips the honeyed wine from her Yeti tumbler. She is taking three European history courses and sinks low into the seat, tries to look mean, tries to feel drunk. She hasn't yet been able to open a book about herself; instead, she wants to understand how the men speak of her — if she is mentioned at all.

Men. These men. Men that make excuses, take all the credit with swords, with swinging ropes, with crude rhymes like: Divorcedbeheadeddied, divorcedbeheadedsurvived.

She supposes times have changed, though can't necessarily say if the fight is better.

On Saturday nights, Anne bartends at a local tavern. She chose the job based solely on the uniform. Though tavern wench isn't the right costume for the time period she remembers, nor for her class, it's the closest she can get to her roots. She logs drink orders to memory: wine, beer, Sex on the Beach, Manhattans; shake, pour, repeat. On smoke breaks, she escapes to the alley. There, she takes a shot of mead. She likes the way it warms her insides, reheats her memory. When her boss, Hank, says, "What you drinking?" Anne says, "Have a sip." He does, and she smirks at his grimace.

Anne thinks of her own Hank. How love was good at first, how she waited seven years to be Queen, how he broke the church for her. In the dark of the alley, she traces a line across her throat, remembering the way Henry used to kiss her pulse with hot lips — gentle when he loved her, hungry when he hated her. And her own mouth, the way it murmured prayers over a book with razor-thin vellum pages, the way it did not tremble — no, never, not once — on the day of her execution when she repeated, "to God I commend my soul."

At least the cut from the sword was quick and clean.

She glances over to catch Hank staring.

And because she throws no man a bone, she turns on her heel, lifts her skirts, and leaves him and his mouth in a kind of gonzo-gawp. "Boy, bye," she says.

Sunday morning, she rises. She dresses, packs her lunch, her bible, her tumbler of mead, and leaves her dorm room. As she walks, she pictures Henry again — ruddy and orange and fit. She supposes he is out there, somewhere. A reincarnated boy ready to marry, ruin, do it again. Fuck, marry, kill; isn't that how the game goes these days?

When Anne enters the church, she imagines them meeting.

The now-Henry will be new and fun but still six-foot-one with a legendary waistline. They will have drinks in a very public, very expensive place. Henry will take her hand, clasp it to his broad chest, apologize. "I want to try again," he will say. And his booming voice will make Anne look at him through lowered eyelashes.

Anne will wonder at their future, knowing their past.

She will lean away from him, smiling with a patience she's kept since the platform of her execution. From her backpack, she will pull her tumbler of mead and pour two glasses. When a pretty young waitress catches Henry's eye, and he glances over his shoulder, Anne will add the poison.

Henry will take one last look at the waitress, look back at Anne, and ask, "What say you?"

And Anne, thinking, *Kate and Anne and Jane and Anne and Kate...* She finally will say: "I'll drink you for it."

Cheap Tanya

He wrote my name in the stars. Connected the dots of the constellations until his index finger spelled out *Tanya*. It was romantic. A starlight billboard, backlit by black, splashed with my moniker. "Tanya," he said, and I watched the way his mouth moistened, how he worked the word over with a fat, red tongue. James was honest like that. He said fancy things. Touched me in fancy places. I loved it.

The rain fell warm as bathwater, but the cement was even warmer. I rolled up onto the balls of my feet — not to get away from the heat; to embrace it. I got close to James' mouth. His breath was like a sunset: juicy from orange Fanta and lazy with his south Texas drawl. He liked to pretend he was a cowboy. He had a motorcycle and a polished belt buckle with guns on it. Sometimes when we laid together, I liked to pretend we were one. I'd press my body to his, imprinting the cool steel from the buckle into a soft spot on my abdomen. I'd roll my bony hip over it, bursting blood vessels. James' skin was like iron. I wanted it to brand me.

"If we go, we'll have to live in cheap motels."

"Good," I said. "I can do cheap. I can do motels. Long as I have you."

He stared at me. Ran a thumb across my sharp jaw. I felt the imprint of his nail — massive moon marks — as he pressed hard like he couldn't believe I was real. Like I was Bonnie and he was Clyde. My heart beat like a pulpy drum inside my chest. I wanted him so badly to agree to take me with him.

I bit down on his bottom lip, fat like whale blubber. I felt the skin split. Blood and salt ran rivers into my mouth. James kissed me hard, then spat the muck we shared on the ground. It mixed with the mud and the rain until it looked like cold, mushy leftovers.

"I have to go." His finger brushed feather-light against my cheek. "Mom wants me home for dinner."

I watched him hop on his bike. Red taillights disappeared around a corner like jolly Christmas lights. I sank down into a squat. The soles of my feet were like two lonesome organs looking for an invitation to roam. *Come and get me*, I thought. *I'll be here. Ready and waiting to go.*

Far Away from Everywhere

The billboard says the end is near. Dad believes it. He takes us to the bank, withdraws all the money we have — life savings drained, college fund gone. He's out of a job, and then we're out of hot water. We sell everything. Dog, drapes, dishes. We sell our house, too. I say goodbye to every wall, to the silky rosebud wallpaper. Mica and I climb our treehouse one last time, and I don't even mind the splinters. I wish they'd stick around a little longer.

After that, Mom piles the cash into a briefcase, an old, battered one she found at the Salvation Army. She says it feels cooler that way. She looks cool, too. Big, fancy sunglasses on her face. Her dark wig piled in a swirling bun. Spy-like. She better look cool because cancer does not matter now.

Dad takes the cash to Jonas. Jonas predicts fire and brimstone. We've known him for years. Followed him from our church to his. Lately, he's become news. A big deal. Mom likes to clutch at his robes, kiss his glittery rings. For someone who claims to be poor, he sure smells a lot like money. Jonas counts the cash, embraces Dad. Now we have a campervan.

Our campervan joins the caravan. A throng of Jonas's followers journeying across the country to spread the good word. At least that's what the press release says. California to Arizona to Texas. Like Johnny Cash, we've been everywhere, but everywhere doesn't matter because we're going nowhere. On busy Main Street corners, me and Sissy Bowers hand out doom-and-gloom pamphlets. The end of the world is coming! Sell everything! Be free!

Our campervan rattles like a tin can in a windstorm. It's cookie-cutter, the inside cramped. Dinettes. Plaid curtains. A pump sink and a stove. A removable table that can be turned into a bed, or a shield. I hate it. I'm cold all the time. I miss school. I miss Jeremy McBride. He'd try to kiss me under the bleachers, and I'd sock his arm until it bruised. The one friend I've made here, Sissy, all she does is stare at the sky and mutter about how she'd kill for some kombucha. She wants her old life back, too. I miss hot water. Water that comes from a sink and not a bucket. "It's an adventure," Mom tells us. "Until September sixth," Dad laughs, elbowing her bony rib. Mom's expression is placid. Mica buries her face in her pillow, crying.

The sixth of September turns to the seventh, and we are still here. But not Mrs. Coxon. She hanged herself with a shoelace because there was no fire in the sky. And yet, Jonas still has a job. No one pulls the billboards. More go up. A new date is announced. Only a year is given. I calculate the time on my fingers, sticky with almond butter. In four years, I'll be eighteen. I used to think that was the perfect age to start running, but I know better now. The anger in my body buzzes like bees. They want to escape, to pour out of my mouth all at once.

"I need milk, Daddy," Mica says. Her cheeks are sunken. She looks hungry, so I give her my thin sandwich. Two scrappy pieces of bread with a meager slather of jelly. She chomps into it, and soon her spelling workbook is stained with cherries. Dad says, "I don't want to talk about milk. I want to talk about the weather. Look at those clouds. They are mushrooms of doom." "It's three years away, Harold," Mom says with a peaceful smile. She's pulling out strands of her remaining hair and making a tic-tac-toe grid on the dinette table. Deathbed board games are all her rage. "Want to play?" she asks me. "How can you smile?" I ask her. I grip a marker in my right hand. I can see it in her eyes; she'll be dead in a year. "How can you not?"

I go in search of milk for Mica. I don't understand these people, the way they buy it. They believe but in a scary way. In an *or-else* way. Desperate eyes like hungry dogs for a bone that isn't being thrown. When the cops come to remind us about the overnight camping rules, my father lies as good as Jonas, and they leave without us. They leave us with Mom and Dad. I want a home again, but I want a home without these people. I imagine me and Mica somewhere better, in a bedroom with flowered wallpaper and soft lights and blankets without holes. My sister has all the milk she wants. And me, maybe I have a bathtub with hot water.

In Oklahoma, we have Sunday service on the prairie. Our caravan circles like covered wagons. Tall grass sways in the breeze. The sky is gray like Dad's tooth. Mom skips because she's too sick to sit on milk crates and buckets. I skip out, too. Down by the river, I run into Sissy. She's three campervans over. Hers always smells like sausage, her Dad out front at the grill, waving a kielbasa on a stick, yelling like Oprah, "Come and get a piece! And you, come and get a piece too!"

We say hey, then we climb the stacked logs near the bank. "Beavers," Sissy says and points. I pretend I'm back in my treehouse, and when I've reached the highest peak — which isn't very high at all — I angle my head back toward the swaying tall grass. Over the wind, I hear Jonas's voice as loud as a bullhorn: "We are at the end! There is no existence for an unsaved soul!" I inspect my palms for splinters. "They're idiots," I say. "Does anyone really believe this billboard bullshit?"

"Let them believe," Sissy says, and lights a match.

Tomorrow, Grandma picks us up from the shelter. Mica and I are headed to her cookie-cutter house in Phoenix. Best of all, it's hot there. It will be hot.

Everlasting Full

Cold, only cold; hungry, always hungry. Only after she met and ate Eddie did Elizabeth begin to warm up.

She never was fed as a child. Went for most of her young life with low body fat and pangs of insatiable hunger. Would study the way her bony hands turned blue and venous, fingertips bulbous and icy to the touch, skin paper-fine and milk-white. A mother who likened sin to food, who thought a hot meal was cause for guilt, kept the luxury of food at bay. Meager scraps — just enough to quench the stomach pains — were given to her. And so, because of this, she got to know her body well. Every last ache gurgling within her empty bowels, knees and shins and shoulder blades shark-finning the sheets as she curled up into herself, going to bed hungry. She slept with a plate beneath her pillow, and at night she'd tuck her arm into a little wing underneath her head, her palm touching the cool china under the feather pillow, and she'd swear that one day she'd never go hungry again. Somehow she'd find a way to stay full — everlasting full.

"No pitties, no kitties, no beards, no bartenders," she writes in her online dating profile. Chefs. She'll only accept chefs. Elizabeth knows it's a dicey business. Chefs barely have time for a pet, let alone a woman to love. But, as she types, she knows she wants a man who won't stop cooking until she's well fed. She posts a picture of herself, a daisy in her hair, standing outside of the New York Public Library, her librarian badge hidden underneath her wool sweater. She's skinny and flat-chested, but she has a lovely smile, and it's less than 24 hours before she gets her first response.

She meets him at a gastropub wearing a heavy cardigan. Twice, she's asked the bartender to turn down the air conditioning, but her requests have gone unanswered. He stands when she arrives, gently but confidently shakes her hand. Instantly, Elizabeth likes the meaty weight of his palm, the heavy, hot, comforting feeling it gives to her. He orders scotch and is surprised when she does the same. It's been her drink for such a long while, filling her belly, keeping it warm when nothing else could.

Eddie is meaty like his palm. He wears a goodly stomach, sports a piebald 5-o'clock shadow and has hairy knuckles. He dons a buffalo plaid shirt, jeans and the typical shoe of chefs: Crocs. All these things Elizabeth finds attractive. He does not look hungry, and when he orders a pork belly appetizer her mouth begins to water. Her knees go weak, weaker still when he slides a fork her way and tells her "dig in."

Elizabeth grips the fork, knuckles white. She forgets how many appetizers they polish off. But she'll always remember that first one – the pork belly. She imagines telling their children how they met. "Over a belly of pork," she'd laugh. They'll serve it at their wedding; order it every anniversary. And it will still never taste as good as the day they first met.

Elizabeth loves Eddie because he feeds her, and Eddie loves Elizabeth because she eats what she is fed.

She waits with sweaty palms, with mouth salivating, and watches with longing to see what's set before her. Hearty dishes like pot-au-feu, boeuf bourguignon, quail terrine. She tears at the food hungrily, licking butter-coated lips, loving the way the fork tines sound on Eddie's fine china. She lives for fleur de sel nestling into her cupid's bow, turbinado sugar sticking in the corner of her mouth, or dark cocoa dusting her fingertips.

A normal weight returns to Elizabeth, her hips rounding nicely, her breasts slightly heavier. Gone are the heavy cardigans, the pilled sweatpants. Elizabeth can tempt tank tops, bristling only somewhat when she encounters a draft from a window or air conditioner.

And on those nights when Eddie is home and the kitchen is cooling off, when she gets on her knees and takes Eddie in her mouth, she's never felt so full.

The ring is a yellow diamond., like a cut of hard cheddar.

She will plan for the dress (a mermaid cut to accommodate her new curves) and pick a venue (somewhere outside, but it must be in the afternoon so she can be warm in the midday sun) but the food — the cuisine — is up to her chef.

Elizabeth listens with bated breath as Eddie describes the caterer he's planning to hire. "Canapes galore!" he cries, and, unable to help herself, Elizabeth clasps her hands together in childlike glee. The cake will be vanilla, five layers covered in whipped buttercream and decorated with a string of edible pearls. Elizabeth pictures this. Pictures being finger-fed a moist piece of wedding cake and letting the creamy frosting slip and slide across her tongue.

Elizabeth bristles with pride in the presence of their new apartment, especially the kitchen. It near brings her to tears. Pots and pans hang over the stove. A butcher block of knives, a full spice rack, a marble cutting board. She imagines the meals her husband will cook here, the food that will fill her belly.

Six months into their marriage, Eddie breaks bad news at breakfast, over corned beef hash and eggs Benedict (both of which she'll never eat again).

Unprepared for his announcement, Elizabeth wrings a cloth napkin between her hands as Eddie explains he's retiring from chefdom to become a doctor. Horrified, she listens as Eddie details the situation: cooking was merely a hobby until he discovered his *real* calling; now it's back to school for seven years where he'll still work with his hands and with knives, only now saving lives instead of filling bellies.

Eddie teases, "Don't worry, my little hangry one, I will still feed you."

Elizabeth says, "Don't," and turns away. She does not take kindly to anyone making fun of her hunger, not even

her husband. His words do nothing to alleviate her fears –
the sheer betrayal of it all. This is not what she wanted.
Elizabeth asked for a chef. Her dating profile had specifically
stated it. She *required* a chef.

She told herself she hadn't been meaning to use it. But
then it was just a dash and then another, and then Elizabeth
found herself pouring a heaping tablespoon of rat poison
into Eddie's coffee.

She watches the mug steam, debating, and then she
remembers her online ad and how it was answered with a
lie. Decided, Elizabeth gives the coffee a hearty stir and then
calls her husband down for a breakfast she has cooked.

The twitching stopped a little more than an hour ago.
She was sad to see him go. Eddie: the only one she ever
loved; the only one who had ever fed her. So it seems only
right she should feed on Eddie, so that he makes her full one
last time.

Kneeling beside her husband, Elizabeth brandishes
Eddie's chef knife — a large, weighty object, the steel glittery
in the kitchen light. Eyes to his thighs, she makes a notch —

a tiny cut really—and, ignoring the blood, ignoring everything else except her hunger, she cuts and carves and cuts and carves and then it's done.

She prepares a pan on the stove, dials the heat up high, and, after a good three minutes, adds a pat of butter and some chopped garlic like she's seen Eddie so often do. The oil sizzles and spatters, and Elizabeth adds the piece of meat. Briefly, she sears it on each side, but not too long for fear of making it leathery. When it's done — a perfect golden brown color — she lets it cool. And then she cuts a perfect piece. Only a nibble, really.

She sheds her cardigan as she eats, her bare arms hot, flushed even. A warmth spreads throughout her body, one she's never felt before. Delighted, Elizabeth giggles aloud in that quiet kitchen. Oh, how Eddie tastes like what she's been fed on. Truffled risotto, cheesy poutine, buttery foie gras, and — let's not forget — salty pork belly.

Fed and finished, her stomach swollen, she holds its roundness beneath her palms, feeling the fullness within.

Eddie — he's everything Elizabeth had always wanted.

Backseat Blues

It's Mama's car. A big boatload of a machine, the '65 Chevy Impala is. The only thing she ever bought with her own money until Daddy got hold of her.

Mama always drives. Daddy always gets the passenger seat. And I always take the backseat. Mama loves Daddy more than me. But I don't mind.

Sometimes I love Daddy more than me, too.

When I'm young, Daddy and I have a conversation:

"Mama gets sad, Maybelline. You know that right?"

"I do, daddy."

"And if she's ever sad around you, you come get me, you hear?"

"Yes, sir."

Daddy swats a mosquito away. He reaches over to squeeze my knee, the knobby bone wattling under his palm. "You're a good girl."

Sometimes, when Daddy isn't working, the two of them take the car out. Mama blows me a kiss, Daddy a wink, before climbing into their respective spots.

They never tell me where they go, but they come home giggly and smiling.

I know, though.

Mama's blouse smells faintly like the lilacs that grow down by Chesser's Pond: a mossy overgrowth of scummy water. Kids at school use it as a place to neck and pet.

They stumble through the front door, stop in the middle of the kitchen and just dance. Daddy hums some tune only Mama recognizes. She stands on the tops of his feet, both of them swaying back and forth, reeds in a light breeze.

Mama dances on Daddy's toes until the sun rises.

We're sitting in wicker, relegated to the porch after one of Mama's spells, the ice cubes in my lemonade clinking together as I take long, deep gulps. Daddy wipes sweat from his brow and cradles his beer.

"Why'd you save her, Daddy?" I ask.

I always ask this, phrase it nicely on honest nights, when all I really want to know is why he ever married someone as crazy as her.

His response never wavers. "She needed savin'. We both did."

I just sip my drink.

We expect Mama to cry when Daddy gets the letter. Instead, she grits her jaw and fires up a batch of eggs over easy. Daddy watches her back quiver as she stabs the runny yolks.

He takes my hand when she snaps, "Are you coming to breakfast or what?"

"Don't leave me here alone" I whisper.

"You'll be alright. Just listen to your mama."

"She never liked me. She likes you better."

Daddy dips his forehead to mine. He kisses my cheek, brushing the hair out of my face. His palms shake.

She drives him to the base. I stand on the porch and wave goodbye to taillights.

He is all she talks about.

From the movie we can't see because Daddy wanted to, to the dinner we can't cook because it's his favorite meal. I want to ask, "What about me? What about me, Mama?" Instead, I go sit on the porch and wish for something I shouldn't be wishing for.

I catch Mama ripping up coupons in the middle of Aisle Two in front of the bread and English muffins.

"Mama, what are you doing?"

"C'mon, Maybell, we're going."

"But. The milk-"

"We don't need milk! Don't you see? We have milk."

I think of the empty fridge at home, but keep quiet.

Mama gets a letter and begins humming Daddy's tune. She smiles. She takes me in her arms, and we sway. I breathe in her soft scent and am surprised when her blouse smells like lilacs

I answer the door. Two uniforms stand there with solemn faces, jumpy eyes. "Is your mother home?" one asks.

It sounds like a trick question, but I call for her anyway. The thumping of my heart can be heard in my ears. Mama rounds the corner, stopping in the middle of the hall when she sees them. She lets loose a wild keen and flees upstairs. Her bedroom door ricochets shut; photos rattle on the wall.

She cries at night. I bury my head under my pillows so I can't hear her scream into hers.

A week later, we drive out to Chesser's Pond. Even without Daddy around, I still crawl into the backseat, the vinyl squeaking a protest. Mama says, "Lock your door," and pulls her seatbelt tight.

Magnolia trees wave at us as we drive tar streets through town before winding up on the dusty gravel back road. The Impala descends down the sloping hill, the glistening pond waiting in the periphery. Mama wheels into a spot with a perfect view of the mossy green water. She leaves the car running.

It runs for a long time.

My leg bounces. My fingers move to the shiny, metal lock.

The voice is crisp. "Don't you dare touch that knob, Maybell." My nubby fingers stop their forward march. We wait some more in the idling car. I put a hand on the window, pressing flat against the shiny cool glass, a fortune teller's palm on a crystal ball. It's hot, and after a long while I ask, "Can I get out now, Mama?"

Wrapping an arm around her headrest, she twists around. She looks through me, at the door, at the heat outside. She faces forward again, placing both hands around the steering wheel.

"Okay, baby."

I jerk the lock up, throw the door open wide, and tumble out of the backseat.

Mama rolls down her window. "Daddy left us some money in the Folgers's can under the sink."

With that, she puts the car in gear and punches the gas. The Impala hits Chesser's Pond like an iceberg, and for a moment I almost think the old Impala will float, but then Mama and the car sink beneath the mossy surface, my greasy palm print still on the window, life line and heart line smudged against the glass.

Garbage Girl

It's trash day. I know it by the cramps in my belly. Not the calendar on the fridge. Or the City of Evanston's website. Or my mother's finger poked in the face of my father as a reminder to take out the trash because last night's rotisserie is starting to smell.

Once a month, ever since I turned twelve, my cycle's synced to the sound of the garbage truck. Not the full moon or the new moon or the tides. I cramp and menstruate on trash day. But I can't make a peep to anyone, because I'm just a garbage girl in a recycling world.

From my bedroom window, I see the solid waste services truck outside, hear the awkward clang of its arm against plastic cans. Aching cramps pulse in my hips, my lower back. The trash can is hauled high and then dumped. Right on schedule, I bleed.

My mother takes me to the doctor. I tell him about the pain in my belly. When he opens his mouth to give a diagnosis, my mother interrupts him. To me, she says, "The technical term for it is the abdomen. Use medical terminology, Lucy. Use your brain." She takes my hand, presses it lower, near my hip bone, the curve of my pelvis. She slaps my flesh. Hard. She does it again. She sounds it out, says, "This is your ab-dough-man. It's where your cramps live. It's where you try to be a woman. Make yourself one if you can."

The doctor watches from a corner. He prescribes only a muted smile. It's the same one my father wore when he left, because — no shit, buddy — my mother's awful.

My cycle has changed. Sometimes the cramps arrive on trash day. Sometimes they come at the strangest of times, like when my mother says to keep it the fuck down or get out of her face. Or the time I overhear a slice of President Trump's speech on TV. Or the day Molly McGrew laughs and announces to the class that my father really ran off with a barmaid. I take a swing at her head; the blood starts to gush out of me. Teachers gather. "She's fine," I tell them. "She's not the one bleeding."

I Google, *what is the definition of trash?*

From dictionary.com:

1. anything worthless, useless, or discarded; rubbish.

2. foolish or pointless ideas, talk, or writing; nonsense.

3. a worthless or disreputable person.

Milo, a boy from English class, kisses me, says he loves me. He touches me in nice places and shows me the messy tattoos on his hairless body. The shamrock for luck, the heart for his dead sister. The bed is soft, the room warm, and we take off our clothes. I lean in and bite at his lip very gently. And then I begin to bleed all over the bed. I am early, not due for another week, so perhaps this is a sign. Milo draws back, his face made miserable by nature. "You ruined the mood," he says, and I tug on his hair and say, "You're right, but it's better than getting ruined by you."

I come to think of my period as a little friend who tells me a monthly secret. When the boy with long hair promises forever, or a piece of litter blows across the ground, or when a college friend promises to pay me back — or when I visit my mother one weekend and she tells me to remember the time she almost ran me over ("Just think about that, Lucy. Think about that..."), and all I can do is picture shoving her down the staircase, shoving a tampon down her loudmouth gullet — I take a breath. I close my eyes. I use my body. I let it work for me, let it get me out alive.

Pads and tampons won't cut it any longer. Instead, I sit on the couch, bleeding alone, a rag between my legs, and ruin my pajamas. I send my professor an email. I ask to retake the chemistry test next week. If I leave the house, I'll drown the world. I watch my marmalade-colored kitten paw at the front door, hear the rumble of the garbage truck. Usually, I'd make my way out to the sidewalk to wave at Ned, my residential curbside collector, and he'd say, "Lovely Lucy, how's your new kitten? Does she still cry at night?" And I'd say, "No, not today. Not anymore."

Over coffee, my father apologizes for leaving. Though it is my time of the month, I do not bleed (it holds off until later when a customer at the pharmacy claims he never received his Xanax prescription), and I accept his apology. This worries me because I wonder if I rely too much on my body if I try too hard to gauge the garbage of the world with my gut. But I know this is what the world wants me to do: trick myself out of trusting myself, so it can be the last piece of trash to touch you.

The tattoo artist frowns at the drawing I hand him. He's handsome with a scruffy beard and bedhead-like hair and wears a bowling shirt embroidered with the name Scott. He says, "Is this...?"

"A tampon," I finish. I point near my hip bone. "But it's a friendly tampon, with little arms and legs and a smile and everything."

The tattoo artist laughs. It's a laugh I want to crawl into. Earlier this week I saw him standing beneath the awning of the tattoo parlor. I liked the delicate way he flipped his butterfly knife back and forth, and now I want to see the way he wields a tattoo pen.

I ask, "Can you do it?"

He stares at me in awe. His eyes — a beautiful chocolatey brown — crinkle. He grins, says, "I can do anything. Where do you want it?"

I hear my mother's voice in my head. Abdomen. Interrupting. Like I knew she would.

"Right here," I say. I pull up my shirt, jerk down the waistband of my jeans. I give my skin a light slap. "Right on my belly."

The tattoo artist leans down. He studiously examines my stomach, up close and with fervor, runs petal-soft fingers over my hip bone. "This looks good," he says, and his breath is so warm against my skin, he could steam open my ovaries.

On our wedding night, my husband dances me across the threshold of our honeymoon suite. His palm brands the small of my back. His hand curls around mine like smoke from a fire. Scott says, "Remember that time I gave you a tampon tattoo and when I was finished, you cried?" It was two years ago, but of course, I remember. I kiss his lips, slip my hands into his pockets. "You made me happy," I say. "With you, I knew I could always wear white."

I Google, *What to do when the trash collection service is interrupted?*

Before bed, my daughter eats slices of Satsuma orange and drinks warm milk dashed with cinnamon. She strips off her pajamas, runs around the table naked. I crouch beside her. A tendril of juice runs down her pale Buddha belly. I wipe it away. All that innocence, all that wild. I suck the sweetness from my finger.

"Do you love my tummy, Mama?" she asks, rising on tiptoes to loop light arms around my neck.

"To the moon and back," I say, telling her a line that is not mine as I watch Scott roll the garbage can to the curb for tomorrow's collection. A red sun backlights him, and I feel the way the blood collects hot down below, the way it readies itself for another day of trash.

My L.A. Jerry

I'm twenty-two when my husband tells me we're leaving our vapid Iowa lives for the bright lights of Los Angeles. He traded his job in plastics out east for some job in plastics out west.

Buck leans in the doorway, cradling ham hocks for elbows, sweaty and apologetic and miserable.

I'll never forget how my mother used to grab her thighs and show me the bundles of fat she thought were stored there.

"You're a stand-up angel," Jerry says, gripping hard on the lighter. I arch forward, gasping, writhing in the passenger seat of the Cadillac as he holds the flame against the small of my back.

When I'm done, I straighten up and breathe, "I wish you had a dick wrapped in razor wire. Maybe then I could leave you alone."

Jerry unzips his pants. Our last night together before I leave for California.

Nobody needs another salesman in Los Angeles. When my husband starts stuttering at the dinner table about the low wages and the dead-end jobs, all I can think about is handing him a buttery dinner roll and suggesting he mop up the sweat on his brow with it. I'm bored here. I need a job. Need to find my L.A. Jerry.

Buck leaves me to the dishes and goes to do better and finer things, like perving in Internet chat rooms.

At the Museum of Death, I've landed a sweet front desk gig asking guests if they'd like to go into the Suicide Room or the California Death Room first.

I dust framed photos and standing cases holding the correspondences and the fine art of serial killers raised on high: a colorful painting of The Seven Dwarfs by John Wayne Gacy; letters from the Nightstalker, chicken scratch of an enraged scrawl bleeding down the page.

A steady supply of smelling salts is on hand. People faint by the baker's dozen every week. I hash mark a tally on a small notepad indicating which room does them in. So far, the Mortician & Funeral Room is in the lead. Apparently staring caskets and body bags in the face is more than what humanity bargained for.

The girls come in groups, talkative and bushy-tailed. Eager and investigative, they maintain a respectful yet loud distance away, gawking at macabre photos and severed heads.

Most men who come are a strange breed. Shifty-eyed, keep-close-to-the-walls, breathe-through-their-mouth kinds of men. I notice the ones who adjust their pants in the presence of the Black Dahlia morgue photos, the ones who surreptitiously wipe clammy palms on the thighs of their slacks.

They intrigue more than worry me, those who would probably rather help you hide the body or see you in the trunk of their car before they ever join the ranks of what society considers normal.

Sharp and lean, I've noticed him — his weekly visits, his keen blue eyes. There's a longing behind them, a quiet and careful wanting.

He brings a gift shop book to the counter, a glossy tabloid type detailing the seedy underside of Hollywood murders. "Anything else?" I ask. Shaking his head, he peels cash from his wallet, deposits it on the counter as I ring up and wait for a receipt.

"No bag," the boy says, and I stop. "For you." Placing light fingertips on the book's cover, he slides it my way.

My husband grunts, shifting his position on the couch, plate balanced precariously on his crotch, the cracked leather permanently molded to his ass. The air reeks of the leftover tuna noodle casserole he heated up minutes earlier. Frowning, he lowers the volume on the TV, noise from next door interrupting his rerun of *COPS*.

I glance up from the book, away from photos showing the severed torso of Elizabeth Short.

Breathy sounds filter through the thin walls of the apartment. They're soft at first, and then quicker, more insistent, like love on speed dial. I shut my book, keeping a finger in its spine to mark my place. The tips of my husband's ears go pink.

Leaning over, I mute the TV and we listen to the woman climax.

The boy is back with coffees. He slides a cup of warm comfort into my palm, asks if I've read the book.

I say I have. I show him my tattered and dog-eared copy. He'll wait for me after work, he says. There's a drive we need to take.

My knee bounces in anticipation. Nothing says romance like a dismembered headless torso. I nod. With a smile and a drum of knuckles on the countertop, he goes.

I take a whiff of a smelling salt just to be sure I'm still on this earth. My nasal passages burn.

We drive around Benedict Canyon listening to "L.A. Woman." We park next to where the late Sharon Tate's house used to be. She was so blonde and beautiful and pregnant. I shrug out of my underwear, knees and shins bumping the bottom of the glove box. The boy wants me to call him Charlie; instead, I think of Tex Watson before his gentle hand finds me in the dim light of the cab.

Contents of a Letter Found on a Stained Bar Napkin

You know I think about you often. The way the edge of your coat was caked with mud. Mud that reminded me of chocolate icing, and then I instantly felt stupid for the thought. Because what was going to happen next would be a lot more serious than chocolate cake. You left soggy footprints on the wool rug, and I winced. I winced, and then I ran. At least I tried to. But you already know all this. I don't know why I'm explaining it to you. You know. I should tell you what you don't know.

Like when you told me you only wanted money, you promised you wouldn't hurt me, your throat closed up and your voice cracked. Not the most flattering tell, but that's when I knew you were a liar. I heard you rummaging through my kitchen drawers looking for a knife.

I knew that when I sat mute and motionless on my couch for two hours you were still in the room with me even though you wanted me to believe you were gone. When I whimpered, you exhaled. I felt your hot breath brush across the back of my neck.

I knew when you closed the bedroom window you had opened to get in that you planned to kill me. You were afraid the neighbors would hear my scream. And it was a signal for me to move.

I knew I'd get out of the handcuffs because I have double-jointed thumbs. Lucky me, right? I waited until you left the room — for a glass of water you said — and fear and adrenaline, like an animal thrashing inside me, took over. You did not see me, even as I passed you in the hall as close as a ghost, and walked right out the front door.

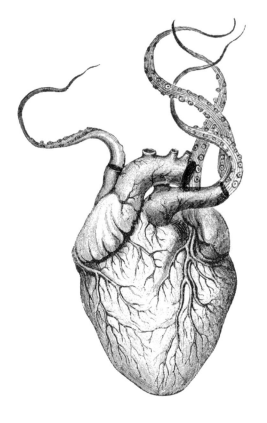

Acknowledgments

Thank you to Josh and the entire Thirty West team for believing in me enough to publish not one, but two, of my books!

Thank you to Carolyn for her gorgeous art that warmed my weird little heart.

Thank you to my friends and family for putting up with my writer rambles. You know who you are.

Thank you to the lit community for being such a warm, supportive, and inspiring place.

Thank you to the journal editors for giving these short stories great homes in the first place, some in earlier forms:

"In-N-Out Doesn't Have Bacon" in *Ghost Parachute*;

"How to Love a Monster with Average-Sized Hands" in *Okay Donkey*

"Hard to Carry and Fit in a Trunk" in *SmokeLong Quarterly*

"The Ice Cream Cone" in *Trampset*

"Guerilla Drive-In" in *PANK*

"The Lie Tree" in *The Toast*

"Prettier Things" in *Pithead Chapel*

"Happiness, Lies, & Reno Rush" in *Pidgeonholes*

"Skillet" in *Five:2:One*

"We Will Set Anything on Fire" in *Maudlin House*

"Cyberspace Soup" in *Crab Fat Magazine*

"Anne Boleyn Could Drink You Under the Table" in *SmokeLong Quarterly*

"Cheap Tanya" in *Lunate*

"Far Away from Everywhere" in *decomP*

"Everlasting Full" in *Literary Orphans*

"Backseat Blues" in *Up the Staircase Quarterly*

"Garbage Girl" in *X-R-A-Y Literary Magazine*

"My L.A. Jerry" in *The Mondegreen*

"Contents of a Letter Found on a Stained Bar Napkin" in *Milk Candy Review*.

About the Author

Jules Archer is the author of the chapbook, *All the Ghosts We've Always Had* (Thirty West Publishing, 2018) and the short story collection, *Little Feasts* (Thirty West Publishing, 2020). Her writing has appeared in various journals, including *SmokeLong Quarterly*, *PANK*, *Maudlin House*, and elsewhere. She lives in Arizona and looks for monsters in strange places. Find her @julesjustwrite or www.julesjustwrite.com